Published by Ad Hoc Fiction.
www.AdHocFiction.com

Purchasing Information:
Paperback available from www.AdHocFiction.com
E-book available from all usual outlets.

Printed in the United Kingdom.
First Printing 2025.

ISBN paperback 978-1-915247-70-4
ISBN e-Book 978-1-915247-71-1

In the Dark Eyes of the Rabbit

by

Debra A Daniel

AdHoc
Fiction

This book is dedicated to my dear, kindhearted grandmother, Po Mama, who fed birds and planted flowers and was the most accomplished worrier I have ever known.

Contents

"The truth is a rabbit in a bramble patch,
and you can't lay your hand on it.
All you can do is circle around and point and say,
'It's in there somewhere.'"

Pete Seeger

In the Dark Eyes of the Rabbit

My father goes hunting. He shoots rabbits.

"I'm not eating that," my mother says. She goes to the bedroom to work crossword puzzles. In the kitchen sink my father cleans a rabbit, its dark eyes shiny as a secret.

***

"I need notebook paper."

"Call the bar," my mother says. "Tell your father to bring some home."

I hate calling. I especially hate when he comes to the phone.

Next morning on my dresser, I find paper.

***

Using our best handwriting my class wrote invitations to our history play.

In the play, I don't say one word. I don't dance the minuet. That's for eight girls and boys with the best handwriting. Our teacher says graceful cursive is dance for your hands.

My clumsy letters slump and stumble. I'm left-handed. Like my father.

During the minuet, I stand in the back, pretending a smile, but really, I'm hunting for my parents. My mother isn't anywhere, but in the back row dark, I find the shadow of my father's face.

***

For the week that my father's sister visits, he's home early every night. My mother doesn't lose herself in bedroom crosswords. We eat dinner together, play Clue, and listen to my aunt's funny stories about my father when he was little. He laughs, making no sound.

***

My father goes hunting but doesn't come home. I even call the bar, hoping he answers the phone. My grandmother whispers prayers and warnings, predicting disaster. We pace. My mother's steps land black and hard. Her sharp eyes flicker. On the sofa I fall asleep. Without a blanket. Without my pillow. It's morning when he returns, empty-handed and smelling like secrets.

***

My father says he lost himself in the swamp. "Snakes slithered," he tells us. "Gators sloshed into the water. In the darkest dark I stayed still as a rabbit."

My mother removes herself. He turns to me.

"Quicksand could've swallowed me. Even my shadow."

I lean toward him, my eyes caught by the shine of his story, by how each stumbling word slants left-handed.

In the Boat with My Father

My father's friend, Red Eye, always invited him to go fishing on his boat, but my father said it wasn't the same. He wanted his own. My family can't afford to buy one.

So every Saturday my father and I searched junkyards till we found two identical 1951 Chevrolets. We bought the hoods and took them home where he welded them together to build a boat.

I was born in 1951 so the boat and I are both twelve years old even though the boat is new-made. My father says he'll name it after me and on its side, we'll paint my name, *Loretta*, in cursive letters on the side.

Once in a fishing contest on the pier at Windy Hill Beach, my father won third place for catching a huge sheepshead fish. My mother said it was ugly. My grandmother said it was dangerous with its big yellow teeth, but my father said he didn't care how it looked and that it wouldn't bite us. Instead we'd bite it, and it would taste delicious.

My grandmother and my mother say they'll never let my father take me fishing in that deathtrap. They tell him that they believe his car hood boat will sink and we'll drown, but he doesn't lose his grin, and he keeps bringing home things for our adventure. Life jackets. Paddles. Shiny, bright colored lures with feathers that will glisten and flick in the water to attract even the most suspicious fish. A new rod and reel. Pink. For me.

My mother won't go fishing. She holds her nose at the smell of fish even when they're fresh caught. When my father cleans them in the kitchen sink, she fusses. She especially hates the way fish stare at her with their dark, glassy eyes.

Once when my father was casting his line, he hooked another man in the eye. He was so sorry that we thought he'd stop fishing forever, but he didn't. The man didn't go blind after all and didn't even blame my father since it was an accident.

Once a fish jumped right out of the water and into Red Eye's boat. My father threw it back. That was an accident, too, he said. He knew the fish didn't do it on purpose.

My father said if every single person went fishing, then the world would be a better place. Fishermen are optimistic, he says, always expecting something good to happen with every cast.

When we're ready to go fishing in the car hood boat, we'll invite my mother to come. We're hoping she'll say yes. My father says we'll keep asking over and over. Even forever, if it takes that long.

In the newspaper I read a story about fish in Texas falling out of the sky. A tornado swooped down on a lake, sucked everything up, and dropped it all on a town like it was raining fish.

I think it would be amazing to run into our yard and pick up dinner, but that wouldn't be fair, my father says. The fish should have a chance, at least. Sometimes, though, when thunder banks build billowy and dark, I see him casting his eyes higher and higher into the sky.

Everyone Calls Me Retta

Unless we're at church or she's introducing me to someone important at the bank where she works, my mother almost never calls me by my real name, Loretta, even though she's the one who insisted that I should carry a glamorous movie star name. She didn't like Greta Garbo or Marlena Dietrich or Rita Hayworth or Lana Turner. They were too high and mighty, she said, and too steamy for their own good.

My father said that any name was alright with him as long as it wasn't Talulah.

My grandmother said it was just asking for trouble to name a baby after a pin-up girl and it, for sure, would lunge me down the road to unladylike escapades. So instead, they picked out a star who was not only beautiful but also friendly, sweet, and charming. Loretta Young. She started out as a movie actress but now she has her very own television show.

I don't mind being named after her. I like the way she sweeps into a room, her chiffon gowns flowing behind her. It's like she is the wind herself. I bet she smells like roses or jasmine or wisteria. On her television show when her theme music starts, she opens the door, glides into her elegant home, comes right up to the camera, and talks straight into it almost like she can see the people watching. Like she can see me.

She's not perky like Annette Funicello or nutty like Lucille Ball or dramatic like Elizabeth Taylor whose names I would've been happy to have, but she seems to want to chat and maybe invite you to sit down and have a slice of cake and a glass of lemonade.

"That would never happen because her television house isn't real," my grandmother says. "It's only a set like a big dollhouse."

"Still I'd like to be on her show," I say. "Maybe she'd ask me to sing."

"I read about a woman who was on television," my grandmother says. She narrows her eyes and lowers her voice. "One of the spotlights fell on her. She got forty-five stitches in her head."

I want to say it would be worth it to be on television, but my grandmother would shame me for wanting to risk harm to my fragile body and delicate life for something so foolish as show business.

That doesn't stop me from readying myself in case my dream comes true. I practice glide-walking into rooms the way Loretta Young does. I wear an old princess costume from Halloween or sneak one of my mother's fancy dresses. I need high heels, but I don't get those until I'm older so I just walk on my tiptoes. I hum her theme music as I float into the room. If I had an audience, they would be sighing in delight and their eyes would be all dreamy.

Sometimes I practice looking into the bathroom mirror as if it's a camera, and I say hello and tilt my head so my fans know I'm sincere and friendly. I open my eyes wide and lift my brows to show I'm excited to see them. I smile and say, "Would you like to join me for strawberry shortcake and some iced tea?"

It would be special if I could meet Loretta Young. She'd hold out her hand to me and say it's lovely to know I was named after her. She'd gush over me and say how elegant I am for such a young girl. Most important of all, she would look deep into my eyes and say my whole name. It would slip from her lips and drift into the air. Soft as velvet. Warm as sunlight. Sounding unique and solid and important. Loretta, she would say. Loretta.

All the Things My Grandmother Hides Away

Coca-Colas. Stashed in closets. Breadbox. Behind fireplace logs. *Life turns hard*, my grandmother says. *Hold something back.*

Scrimped coins. Found pennies. Tugged stingy tight in her velvet drawstring purse. When it adds enough, she buys ice cream from the milkman, but she never eats it with me.

In thunderstorms, she cubbyholes me in the hallway where lightning can't bolt. She tells about sisters herding cows. Struck down. Cows and girls. In a dazzle of bright.

She stories. Girls bathtub-drowning, chicken bone-choking, bicycle-wrecking-neck-breaking. Then she sings hymns about God taking care of us.

My grandmother hides herself, never showing the truth of her. No photographs or scrapbooks to prove there was ever any youngness in her.

But sometimes I pin curl her hair, silvery and silky fine. While I twist and criss-cross and clip, she talks about her girl times. *Lipstick*, she says. *Sassy dresses.* Maybe she's pretending herself a fairy tale.

My grandmother's ears are pierced. Her favorite earrings, tiny milky pearls, hang like whispers just below her lobes. Someday, when I'm thirteen she'll pierce mine. Ice. Needle. Jab. *If you freeze yourself,* she says, *you won't feel anything.*

She'll give me her ruby studs. *Rhinestones, but what's the difference?* she says. *If you believe they're real, they are.*

In a Band-aid box she hides earrings. Wedding band, too. Her knuckles grew too knotted to wear it.

I asked was it real gold. *If you believe it is, then it is*, she says.

Maybe she painted it. Whenever she stews a chicken, she paints the wishbone shiny gold, hangs it in the window, waits for some hope to come true. She never paints with me.

Stay where I can see you, she says. I bring my Barbie into the kitchen, dress her fancy, prance her around. *Too bosomy*, my grandmother says. *Too sassy.*

Sometimes I hide Barbie with the Coca-Colas, hoping my grandmother will smile when she finds the surprise of such a fine lady. I've never seen that happen though.

Maybe, when she's alone in the house, she eats ice cream, drinks Coca-Cola, counts pennies, paints her wishbones. Maybe then my grandmother smiles. Maybe then she believes she's real.

A Photograph of a Chihuahua in a Yellow Coffee Cup and Matching Saucer

Ever since I saw it in a magazine, I wanted it. Desperately. I stared at the chihuahua for hours, kept its picture in my jewelry box, even slept with it under my pillow, I loved every bit of it. Knobby head. Eyes bulgy and bright. Pointy elf ears. Front paws hooked on the cup's rim.

I begged my mother.

"You already have a dog," she said. "You don't pay him any attention."

"Felix smells old. He lives in the backyard. Besides he's not even our dog. The people who lived here before us moved away and left him," I said. "If you ask me, he's not a pet. He's a landlord."

"Retta, honey, nobody asked you," my mother said.

"Dogs bite and give you rabies," my grandmother said. "I knew a mailman who was nipped by a poodle in a tutu. They both died a horrible foaming-at-the-mouth death."

"My chihuahua would never bite me because I'd never dress it up in a tutu," I said.

For months I begged for my chihuahua. On my birthday. On Christmas. As they rolled me away for surgery when I got my tonsils out.

"It's my death bed wish," I said.

"You're not dying, Retta," my mother said. "It's only tonsils. You can have ice cream, but you can't have another dog. You already have Felix."

"Give Felix a chance." That's what my father always said. "Play fetch. Give him treats."

I tried liking Felix. I let him follow me around the backyard. He wagged his tail, but he was too heavy to pick up, too stinky to cuddle. Mostly, he just sat beside me while I read.

"Felix is an okay dog," I told my father, "but he'll never be a chihuahua in a coffee cup.

I almost gave up. Then one Saturday night my father came home late, as usual, but this time, he woke me, holding something close to my face. A rat! I screamed.

"It's your chihuahua," he said. "I won it playing poker."

"Who on earth bets a dog in a poker game?" my mother said.

"I've seen stranger than that," my father said. He handed me the puppy.

"Is it real?" I said, patting its little doorknob head. "Can it sleep with me?"

"You'll roll over and smother it," my grandmother said. She stood in the doorway, wringing her hands, probably already planning the little dog's funeral.

"I'd never do that," I said. "I'll lie perfectly still all night. If you ask me, I think that the happier you are the less you toss and turn in your sleep."

"Nobody asked you, Retta." My mother said my name, *Rrrettta*, like she was ripping off a sheet of aluminum foil. "Besides ladies don't sleep with dogs."She sat on the foot of my bed, her arms folded, her face grinched.

"It has its own bed," my father said. "I won that, too."

That night I had the happiest sleep of my whole life.

***

The next morning my grandmother was making pancakes. I asked her to reach to the highest shelf and get the cup and saucer I'd bought at an antique store last year with my allowance, in case my dream came true.

My grandmother stink-eyed me, but she handed me the cup. My mother, mad at my father for gambling and winning a dog, just kept drinking her coffee and adding more letters to her crossword puzzle.

In the den my father sat on the sofa, puppy on his lap. I put the cup and saucer on the table, fitted my chihuahua inside exactly like the photo, but it trembled so hard that the cup rattled. I picked up the shivery little dog, held it close to my chest until it relaxed.

"How does it feel," my father said, "to get what you've waited for."

I couldn't speak. All my words stayed stuck in my throat. I cuddled up to my father. He put his arm around me.

"I know you're happy, Retta, but look out the window." He nudged me. There, on the porch, sat Felix, his head on his paws, his big eyes droopy and sad. My father said, "Do you know how it feels not to get any attention?"

When my new puppy was sleeping, I went to the backyard. Felix wagged his tail. I gave him treats. We sat together while I read my book. Every few pages I whispered to him. "Good dog, Felix. Good dog."

My Grandmother Brings Coca-Cola

At recess she comes to the schoolyard gate with a full glass. We live across the street so it's not far, even for an old lady. I don't ask her to do it. In fact, it's hard to explain to my friends playing hopscotch. I'm always afraid a teacher will spot her and send us to the principal.

My grandmother says I deserve a treat, but I think she feels guilty for sending me off without breakfast. In the mornings, my mother gets ready for work at the bank, and my father leaves before I'm up. It's my grandmother's job to get me off to school.

But she hates waking early and moving fast. I'm old enough to get myself ready, gather my books. She doesn't have much to do. Except breakfast.

She does prepare it, just not before I have to leave. I could stay and eat, but then I'd be late, and everyone would stare while the teacher scolds me again.

All alone, my grandmother probably eats a lovely breakfast.

Sometimes I make cinnamon toast or eat a banana. My grandmother won't let me use the stove because I might burn down the house. And she won't buy cereal. She says that's a poor excuse for food.

I tell her it's better than nothing when my stomach is growling during math, but she says cold cereal is just giving up.

So she brings me Coca-Cola. I run to meet her. She watches me gulp it down and suggests I come home because the house is too quiet.

I tell her I can't. I want to go back to my friends, but my grandmother looks lonely, so I stay until the bell rings. She walks down the path to our house, and I go to my classroom, my stomach gurgling and unsettled.

Holding on for the Dearest Life

I want to paint my bedroom purple like the peel of a plum. Pink feels silly now that I'll soon be in seventh grade and in a new school.

In the backyard my father looks up at the fallen leaves on our roof. He looks down at me.

I ask if he'll buy brushes and buckets of smooth color. "I'll paint it," I say. "I'll climb the ladder up to the ceiling. I'm not scared."

***

"Ladders bring merciless bad luck, Retta," my grandmother says. She freezes her face, darkens her eyes. "I knew a girl who fell from one," she says, "and was paralyzed."

"My room's so small," I say. "I won't be on the ladder much. I'll tie a rope around myself like a safety belt."

My grandmother's hands swim in cloudy dishwater. Then she pulls the plug. "Now that I think of it," she says, "it was a step stool, and she died, covered in purple bruises."

***

My father climbs a ladder to clean the gutters.

"He'll plummet," my grandmother says, wringing her hands.

I stand beneath the ladder. My father climbs so high it hurts my neck to look up at him.

"Come down," I say. "You'll fall and die."

"You'd be better off," he says, tossing down clumps of damp, rotting leaves.

I hold onto the ladder for dearest life.

"You'd get insurance money," he says. He drops a branch into my grandmother's flowerbed, snapping the stem of one of her favorite dark purple irises.

He comes down. I sigh, relieved, thinking he's done, but he slides the ladder over and climbs again.

***

My father helps me paint my room. My grandmother tugs her chair into the doorway so she can worry closer.

Color overcomes me. "Delicious," I say. "Good enough to drink."

"Drinking paint dries your throat," my grandmother says. "I knew a girl whose throat crusted over and then it collapsed."

My father holds onto the ladder so I can reach the highest places. Before my eyes every trace of little girl pink disappears, and the coming of purple deepens my walls.

What My Mother Says

- Every woman looks better with lipstick.
- You don't need eye make-up, only Vaseline on your brows.
- Marry a man with education and a career.
- Once when I was rollerskating, I broke my tailbone.
- If you press your fingers against your crooked teeth, you can stop them from protruding without using expensive braces.
- Black mascara makes you look cheap.
- Fathers shouldn't stay out late gambling.
- Once, I danced with Gene Kelly.
- High-class men don't wear crewcuts.
- When someone takes your photograph, smile without showing your teeth.
- It's as easy to love a rich man as it is to love a poor one. Maybe easier.
- Too much lipstick is not ladylike.
- Sing with personality.
- Marry a man with clean fingernails.
- Refined ladies never curse or use incorrect grammar.

- If a man stays out late gambling, you know what comes next.
- On your birthday you should thank me for suffering the agony and travail of your birth.
- A toothy grin is not ladylike.
- The best families own mahogany furniture.
- Crossword puzzles make you smart.
- When I was eighteen, a car accident knocked out my teeth.
- My father was the handsomest man in town.
- Once, I won a beauty contest and a trip to Chicago.
- Ladies always carry a handkerchief.
- I dated boys from the best families.
- Once, I sang with a band.
- Good families own a piano even if no one plays.
- To hide your crooked teeth, smile with your lips closed.

The Littlest Angel Teenform Training Bra

To me, the scariest things in the world are my grandmother's breasts. They hang down to her waist. When she takes a bath and gets dressed, she lifts each one up and sprinkles April Violets dusting powder underneath. I've seen her breasts a lot because she doesn't think a thing about walking around naked, and she never wears a bra.

My mother has bought her all kinds. Lacy pink. Heavy-duty thick cotton. Front hook one the color of skin. She nags, but my grandmother refuses even to try one on. So I'm surprised that my mother takes her along to buy one for me.

"It's not ladylike to let your breasts hang loose," my mother says. "Only racy, low-class women would ever consider going without a brassiere."

My grandmother huffs. "They cut off your circulation. I knew a woman whose brassiere suffocated her," my grandmother says. "Vile thing squeezed her like a boa constrictor. I heard the woman's eyes popped right out of the sockets."

"I'm not sure I should get a bra," I say. "It sounds like a deathtrap."

My mother looks in the rearview mirror at me sitting in the backseat, my eyes wide, my mouth open in shock. "We're getting your first bra today," she says. "No arguments."

My grandmother turns her head away and stares out the window. "You're courting disaster," she says.

"Can I get one with cups that stand up by themselves even with nothing in them," I ask, "like the ones you wear?"

My mother glares straight ahead. Her breasts scare me almost as much as my grandmother's. She is flat-chested, like she ordered one extra- small breast and then parted it down the middle. There's nothing there except for two dried-up nipples like raisins. All her bras are padded and pointy. The worst thing that could happen would be if I inherited one breast like hers and one like my grandmother's. Any minute my breasts are going to start growing. There's nothing I can do to stop them. I've had nightmares about that.

What I really want are beauty pageant breasts. I'd also be happy with Barbie doll breasts except that she doesn't have nipples, which could be a problem if I ever have children even though my mother didn't nurse me because I was allergic to her.

***

In the car no one talks again until we get to Berry's Department Store where my mother knows the manager of the children's section, Esther Counts, who has a croaky voice and breasts all puffed up like a bullfrog.

"We need a beginner's training bra," my mother says.

"It's too late to train your breasts. They're a lost cause," Esther says, patting my mother's back and laughing at her own joke.

My mother smiles without showing any teeth. "We want the Littlest Angel Teenform bra, probably the smallest one you have," she says.

"That would be triple A," Esther says. "My granddaughter started in that size, but she's already up to an A. Such an overachiever."

Esther opens a drawer and pulls out bras. She holds up a pink one. It doesn't look like a lady's bra at all, just an ugly, thick, stretchy band of cotton with wide straps. "This is the smallest. It'll probably fit your daughter for a long time, but you'll want to try it on. No refunds on undies, you know."

"Let's go to the fitting room," my mother says.

"No need to waste a room. We'll just pop it on over her blouse," Esther says, talking like I'm not even there. They swoop over me like a flock of gulls and fasten me into that bra before I can run. There I stand in the middle of the biggest store in town with a tight pink bra on top of my shirt.

"It fits," my grandmother says, pushing her way in between them. Quick as a rabbit, she frees me from that bra before anyone could see.

That night after my bath, my grandmother knocks on the bathroom door.

"Change is coming for you," she says, handing me a new box of April Violets dusting powder with a fluffy lavender puff. "You might want this." We look at each other, eye to eye. She shakes her head and sighs. "I don't know that any girl is ever really ready to turn into a woman, but at least, she can smell good."

When she leaves me alone. I sprinkle some powder onto my chest and try on my new bra. Smothering. Hot. Itchy. When I look in the mirror, I feel older and younger all at the same time. A little bit scared and a little bit excited. Not ready. Absolutely ready.

My Grandmother Herself Is Almost an Antique

She collects ladies' snuff boxes, pocket watches, delicate porcelain cups with patterns of flowers, baby spoons. Small things that cost almost nothing.

On Saturdays, my mother drives us to the shabby remains of depot towns that stand sorrowful because trains don't make regular stops there anymore. My grandmother says that it's fine to visit sad places. She says sad places hold the secrets of sad people, and sad people want to rid themselves of the proof of those sad secrets. That's the reason that these old train stations in these old forlorn towns have turned into antique shops.

My mother stays in the car working her puzzle, but I trail behind my grandmother to be there in case she falls. We spend hours examining every knickknack, every rickety chair, every threadbare quilt.

My grandmother heads to the farthest corners where thrown-asides gather in a wobbly pile. She says the best treasures lie hidden in the tumbledown. I don't like the musty dark or breathing in the dust of the dead and gone, but my grandmother hushes me, saying we're paying tribute to the sad losses antiques stand for, that everything we see once belonged to life snuffed out. Still, I can't help feeling like we're in a coffin, and I try not to inhale all that grief.

Once I asked my grandmother how many years it takes for something to be called an antique. "Anything that's been around for a century or more, older even than I am," she said, "but I'm getting close."

She scratched her head and sniffed like she was about to snort. "It would be nice to be an antique," she said. "People pay attention to them."

My grandmother gives attention to old things like arrowheads, stained doilies, and, especially, cast-iron skillets. "Already seasoned. Better than new," she says.

"Never pay full amount," she says, "and if the seller doesn't lower the price, pretend you're leaving without buying a thing."

"Isn't that lying?" I say.

"Ladies don't lie," she says. "They negotiate."

As reward for watching her not fall down, she buys me trinkets. Most of all I love the jewelry: wedding rings, pocket watches, cameos. My favorites are lockets, sometimes with a photograph of someone who was once upon a time loved still inside.

We spend hours hunched over trays of jewelry. My grandmother brings her own magnifying glass so she can discover markings to prove the realness of the gold or almost invisible writings etched into the hidden inside of rings, engravings of everlasting love.

I ask her why she doesn't buy herself a new old wedding band since hers won't fit over her knuckles anymore. She clucks her tongue. "It wouldn't be the same," she says. "The love inside wouldn't be for me."

In the dusty pale light of the antique store we touch each tarnished piece in the display case, telling ourselves pitiful stories of the lost long ago, making ourselves cry at the thought of all those broken hearts. My grandmother says she knew a real girl whose locket held her fiancé's likeness. The young soldier never came back from war. The girl never married. Maybe one day we'll find that very locket, my grandmother and I. She says for that locket, she'd offer full price without a hint of quibble. That way we'd pay tribute to everyone's loss.

Whenever we get back home after a Saturday of being in the antique store, I lift the lid on my jewelry box. The little ballerina unbends herself and starts to dance. I take out my treasures that are older than a century. A silver cross, a baby ring, four heart-shaped lockets, and a thin gold necklace with a broken clasp. I line them up on my bedspread and take time to remember the people who once owned them, the people long, long, long ago gone.

In the Darkest Dark She Takes My Sleep

"Get up," my grandmother says. "It's storming. The lights are out."

I want to say, "Of course, they are. It's the middle of the night," but I don't. She'd tell my mother, and I'd be punished for sassing.

Whenever it storms, my grandmother drags her rocking chair into the hallway where there are no windows. She's afraid to see what's coming. She makes me sit with her until the danger of lightning death passes.

In the dark, she recites her storm rules. No pins in my hair. Lightning searches for metal. No petting my dog. Lightning seeks out animals, even jittery ones like chihuahuas. No going into the bathroom no matter how bad I have to pee. Lightning can burst through faucets and drown you in electricity.

I want to ask why she only wakes me and not my mother who's sleeping in her pink bedroom without my father, who isn't home in the middle of the night storm.

I want to say I have a math test tomorrow and I went to bed reciting formulas for circles—area, circumference, radius—so I won't fail, but now I'll be sleepy and confused by circles that spin me until I'm helpless.

But I don't speak. I sit near the creak of the rocker and listen again to her story about sisters she knew when she was eleven. Sisters struck by a bolt straight out of a blue sky. Sisters who never saw it coming.

"You must watch in bright of day," my grandmother says. "and darkest night, especially then, when no one realizes the lights have gone out and you've lost your power."

The black storm surrounds us. I hold onto my pillow and listen to the pour of rain, the whipping wind, and, from behind her bedroom door, the sleeping hush of my mother.

If Her World Goes Dark

Sometimes I go with my grandmother to her doctors' appointments. Foot doctor for her bunion. Skin doctor for itches. Eye doctor for glaucoma. She doesn't like to go alone, especially not to Dr. Reynolds, the eye doctor. He's the scariest.

He tells her that glaucoma can cause her to go blind. He says she must always, always remember to put her prescription drops in every four hours or she could be in big, big trouble. He says it's very, very important that she must never, never miss an appointment. He needs to keep close, close track of the pressure in her eyes.

Dr. Reynolds says things twice so you know he means business. He puts a special drop in each eye to make her pupils huge and black. Then he sits close to my grandmother, knee to knee, using a big machine to look into and behind her eyes.

Meanwhile I sit in the corner memorizing the letters on the eye chart all the way down to the tiniest row so I can recite them. That way, even if I were to go blind, no one would ever know.

My grandmother is supposed to sit still while Dr. Reynolds tests the pressure in her eyes, but she fiddles, crushing the hankie that she holds in her hand until it is damp and wadded. It bothers me to see her so nervous and even more scared than usual. She holds her breath, bites at her lip, twitches her shoulders until Dr. Reynolds tells her that she is so, so lucky and that her pressure is holding steady, steady as can be.

While we wait for my mother to pick us up, I hold her hand. "If you go blind, don't worry," I tell her. "I'll buy you a Seeing Eye dog."

My grandmother huffs. "I knew a girl whose Seeing Eye dog suddenly went blind while they were crossing the street," she says, "and they both got hit by a bus."

"That's awful, awful," I say, hoping she'll smile when I imitate Dr. Reynolds. She doesn't.

My grandmother is afraid of the dark. She keeps flashlights all over the house so when she can't sleep and wanders around, she can see her way. If she were so blind that even a flashlight wouldn't help, she'd be terrified.

Every time my grandmother gets those special drops, her eyes become super sensitive to light because her pupils are enormous. Dr. Reynolds gives her giant sunglasses.

"These are high, high fashion," he always says and laughs. "You'll look like a movie star."

I look at my grandmother wearing the silly glasses, and I think she's too scared to be a movie star. I wonder how she'd manage if her world went dark. What would it be like not to see the colors of her flowers or know if her clothes matched or where her food was on her plate?

"Would you like to touch my face so you can memorize how I look?" I ask her.

"I know how you look, Retta," she says. "We look exactly alike."

"We do?" I say. I look at her. Her nose is a little lumpy, lips are narrow, her eyes, behind the glasses, are gray blue, and her eyebrows are almost invisible. I don't see me in her at all.

"You look like your mother, and your mother looks like me," she says. "All the women in our family look alike."

My grandmother is totally wrong. My mother doesn't look like anyone I've ever known. She reminds me of a tiny bird that couldn't survive on its own. A parakeet with green feathers. She flits her hands when she talks and spins a curl of her hair around her finger when she sits still. Her bones seem fragile like they might snap if you blew onto them. Her teeth shine like they've been polished, and her eyes are fresh green like the inside of a lime.

I want to tell my grandmother that she must be blind already if she thinks any of us look alike, but that would be mean, mean. Instead, I squeeze her hand and tell her I'll always remind her when it's time to put her glaucoma drops in so she won't have to worry about being in the dark.

My grandmother doesn't say a word, but she squeezes back. "I knew a girl who woke up one morning, and one of her eyes had changed from blue to green," she says. "The doctor said she was fine, but within a week, she was blind."

We stand together. I gaze into the distance, expecting my mother to come for us, but my grandmother stares at the ground, expecting that only the deepest, deepest dark is coming, coming for her.

For Their Own Good We Spy On Our Neighbors

Mavis nips sherry. Walter guzzles beer and curses. That's what my grandmother says, and that's why she won't let me go inside their house.

They argue on their porch. From my bedroom window we eavesdrop.

We scrunch ourselves down. "Isn't spying on them rude?" I say.

"The way they drink, they better wish someone's watching out for them," my grandmother says. "I knew a girl whose drunk parents collapsed. Nobody found them for days. They died from pickled livers."

I'm glad we're looking out for Mavis and Walter. Except for the porch fighting, they're nice to me and they give Felix treats through the fence.

My grandmother and I peek, cracking open the window to hear their fussing.

Today Mavis yells. "My change of life ruined my romantic urges," she says.

"You never had any to start with," Walter shouts.

Mavis hollers. "If you're going to be mean, then

I'm glad my lady-times are done," she says.

"Your shop might be closed," Walter growls, "but that doesn't mean I'm going out of business."

"Then you better find another store," Mavis screams.

"This time I'm leaving for good," Walter yells. He marches off down the sidewalk.

Mavis sobs on the porch swing.

"Shouldn't we help her?" I say.

"Ladies don't pry into other people's business," my grandmother says.

"Mavis won't care. She's done with lady-times," I say. "Besides, doesn't Walter drive a cab? Do they have a business, too?"

"Monkey business," she says.

When Walter comes home, I peep at them. He must've found a store because he brings beers and gives Mavis Hersey's kisses. I watch them go inside, leaving the porch swing swaying.

I run to the kitchen to give my grandmother the news. "Walter's back." I say, "and I don't think Mavis is changing her life after all.

"Women's lives never change," she says, "no matter how much they might hope for it."

She stands at the sink washing the same old pans, wearing her same old apron, a gold-painted wishbone hanging from a string in the window.

Things My Grandmother Told Me

- Wallowing will make you sick and weak.
- Get up even when you don't feel like it, especially when you don't feel like it.
- Life will turn on you when you least expect it, so you had better keep your eyes open.
- Dead soil won't grow anything that lives.
- When I was young, girls weren't allowed to be young.
- Tight clothes cut off your circulation and cause you to think crooked.
- I knew lots of girls who died before they lived.
- The war changed everything.
- Having a baby hurts in a thousand ways.
- The Depression changed everything.
- In every minute there are a thousand scary ways to die.
- Finding a penny is good luck.
- If you can save a thousand found pennies, without spending any, you'll have a thousand days of good luck.

- Getting married changed everything.
- Tight clothes make you bulge out in the wrong places.
- Even before you hear the thunder, lightning can bolt you.
- When you smile in a photograph, purse your lips.
- Dangly earrings are not for daytime.
- If you have to pass gas, don't do it in the kitchen.
- A tablespoon of water can drown a baby.
- A girl can drown in a bucket of water or a kitchen sink or a boat, especially a homemade one.
- If the smell of yourself is good, you can breathe easier.
- No matter how hard you try, sometimes bad luck will find you anyway.
- A girl can drown from the inside.

Flowers That Were Not Born Here

In our backyard, my grandmother and my father fashioned a greenhouse where dozens of plants live in comfy beds, cushioned with rich soil.

"Seedlings need warmth, different from what the sun offers," she says. "They'll die in the cold-alone."

My grandmother knows. She lost a long list of babies. Jeremiah. Rebecca. Benjamin. Ruth. And one more whose name, she claims, she doesn't remember. She's fibbing. Nobody forgets the name of their baby.

I think that unmentioned child is the one she misses most, the very sound of its name must break her heart. She doesn't like to talk to me about the old days, but sometimes, if she gets her hands busy, she'll forget and start telling her life secrets. That's how I know a little bit about my grandfather who, otherwise, might as well be invisible.

After the war when he came home fidgety and hollow inside, he couldn't make decent wages in their farm-cow town so they moved from the home where my grandmother birthed those babies, leaving the cemetery where they lay cuddled together in a single plot.

They were too poor to afford separate graves, not even names on a headstone, only the words *Our Babies.*

On Sunday my grandmother leads me to the greenhouse. Almost like we're praying, we kneel beside the plants. Dampness curls my hair. I hear leaves swaying, almost smell colors lifting into air. I bend toward the breath of my grandmother.

"Name to me all of your children," I say, hoping to unearth the unknown baby.

She sighs. "Your mother was my only child," she says, "my onliest child, my loneliest child." She wedges her trowel into dirt, unsettles clods, loosens the root-bound hibiscus, nestles it into a larger bed.

"But once upon a time you had other babies."

"Not any that lasted," she says.

The cool dirt gentles against our hands, gathers under our fingernails. We mound soil around plants, tamping it down so each tiny stem stands sturdy and straight.

The Worst Secret about My Grandmother That I Will Never Tell Anyone

On Saturday nights my grandmother sits on the edge of the bathtub. She pulls a little stool up next to her with supplies: tissues, flashlight, Q-tips damp with water or Vaseline, and thin, bendable hairpins. Then she calls my name. She's ready to clean my nose.

No matter where I hide, I can hear her voice. Hard-pitched like a crow's caw. Sharp as a claw.

Sometimes if I have a friend spending the night, I beg my mother to tell my grandmother that I don't need my nose cleaned. "I'm not a baby," I say. "I can blow my own nose."

On those nights I get excused from the torture of the ritual, the sicky smell of wet cotton.

If anyone in my class ever found out that my grandmother cradles me on her lap, my body smushed up against her breasts, my spine bent crooked, my head tilted back while she plunges hairpins and Q-tips inside my nose to loosen the dried mucus she believes lurks inside, then I would be teased and bullied and left to sit alone at lunch with no friends at all.

I'd die if anyone found out how she shines her flashlight into the tiny caves of my nose, scraping the floors and walls like she's searching for rabid bats or hibernating bears or buried treasure. If anyone found out, I'd have to become a nun who takes a vow of silence and lives in a convent. And I'd never have a boyfriend or go to a dance or win a beauty contest or become a famous singer.

My nose is small with almost no bridge at all. There's no reason to bother such a tiny thing because there's no room for thick snotty clots that could block my breathing and collapse me into a heap.

I wonder if my grandmother cleans her own nose with such importance like it is her mission in life. Her nose is rounded on the end with nostrils that flair out when she doesn't like something. She keeps a lacy handkerchief stuffed in her sleeve to catch its constant dripping which plops from the top as if, on her, gravity works backwards.

"If I don't clean your nose for you, then it will smell from the inside out," she says. "Worse than bad breath."

"But I can blow my nose," I say. "I'll blow it until all the stink is cleared out of my whole body."

This year I'm in seventh grade. I'm too old to have my nose invaded. When my mother drives me to the junior high school, I beg her to talk to my grandmother. I plead, promising I'll do dishes and take out trash and, most importantly, that I'll keep my own nose clean.

"It matters to your grandmother." That's all she says.

I imagine ways to keep clear from the Saturday night torture. I tell my grandmother that I can't smell anything because my nose has been permanently damaged. I pray for a massive nosebleed right after she finishes to scare her into thinking she's wounded me. I inhale red pepper to bring on a massive sneezing fit. Nothing has ended my shame.

I've endured the nose cleaning for all my years. My mother tells me it won't be forever, that nothing lasts forever, that one day when my grandmother is dead and gone, that I'll wish she were here to clean my nose, that I'll surely wish she had lasted forever.

My mother says that I'll be sorry my grandmother's not here to push the chair up next to my bed so I won't roll out and crack my skull open, that I'll be sorry she's not here to cut my apples into tiny pieces so I won't choke on them and turn blue with death, that I'll be sorry she's not here to forbid me to cross the street without her watching so the bus won't speed around the corner, slam into me and drag me down the hill until I roll off into the gutter.

"Your grandmother loves you," my mother tells me.

"She loves me too much for my own good," I say.

On Saturday night I stand in the bathroom, looking at my miserable face in the mirror, staring at my poor little nose. I flair out my nostrils and turn toward my grandmother where she sits on the bathtub's rim, balancing herself on the edge.

There's Nothing Close to Normal Here

I never really see my parents love each other. Not like the parents in television shows. Situation comedies is what they call them. Not like those shows where the father comes home from work every day at the same time and hangs his hat on a peg and his coat in the closet and looks as fresh as he did when he left that morning. Not like the father who kisses the mother on the cheek and asks what's for dinner and then says, yum, my favorite. Not like the father who goes into his study to count out the daughter's allowance, dropping the coins into her bank shaped like a happy, sunny yellow elephant.

I've never seen my parents hug or kiss. Not like those episodes where the parents go out to dinner or celebrate their anniversary. Not like those shows where they stay up late after the kids are asleep to talk about what funny thing happened at the office or the PTA meeting or those crazy neighbors next door or how they want to surprise their daughter with a puppy or a vacation or singing lessons.

Those shows always have grandparents who come for visits but never stay because they have their own farm or ranch or cottage and like to bowl or play bridge or bake cookies that win prizes at the county fair. Those grandparents still hug each other and dance and hold hands just like the parents do.

That's what happens in those television shows, those situation comedies. Maybe that happens in my friends' houses. I don't know about that. I do know that in our house we have situations, but they are not comedies at all. Maybe those shows are normal, but nothing I've seen in my real life is even close to that.

Like the Family of a Rabbit

For Christmas I got a beginner's magic set. I didn't ask for it, but now that I have it, I want to trick people, amaze them, make things disappear right before their very eyes.

Sleight of hand, that's what the directions that came with the set call it, the art of distraction, how you can make someone see what is and isn't there with the wave of a wand and a mysterious word.

I ask my father why I've never heard of any famous magicians who are girls. He says maybe it's because women have a harder time than men do with the idea of things disappearing. That doesn't make sense to me. Besides, magicians only make things disappear temporarily. If I work at it and become very good, then I could be the first internationally famous girl magician.

I practice and practice, starting with the deck of cards. I shuffle and cut the deck and ask my father to pick one, but not to show me. Then I close my eyes, toss my head back, hum mysteriously, and pretend to hear voices from the great beyond. I open my eyes and tell him he chose the king of diamonds.

His mouth drops open. He nods, amazed. What he doesn't know is that all the cards are the king of diamonds. That seems a little too easy. I can only do that trick one time during a performance or never again if any of the same people are in the audience.

I move on to the harder tricks in the set. There's a plastic woman that I can saw in half with a plastic sword and there's a plastic rabbit that I can pull out of a plastic hat. I tell my father that I think I'm already too advanced for the beginner set, that maybe I need a real sword and a real rabbit.

He says that sawing a real rabbit in half is a lot harder and could be messy if I'm not careful.

"I'm not going to saw the rabbit in half," I say. "I'm going to pull it out of a hat and then make it disappear into thin air, but only temporarily. I need a real rabbit for that to be a showstopper."

I am telling him this while we are on our way to church, the only place we ever go as a family: my mother, my father, and me. My grandmother never goes to church. She says she's memorized the important Bible verses already and knows all the hymns so she doesn't need to go anymore. Also she doesn't like to dress up in tight clothes and shoes. While we temporarily disappear, she stays home and eats cornbread mushed up in buttermilk.

On the drive to church I'm in the back seat. In the front seat, my mother looks in the mirror of her compact to make sure her lips and cheeks are not too gaudy for Sunday. "Rabbits are not good pets," she says. "They're not ladylike."

"I'm not asking for a pet," I say. "I'm asking for a business partner."

My father lights another cigarette. My mother rolls the window down and fans the air around her face.

"Maybe the next time you go hunting, you could capture a rabbit for me," I say.

"Rabbits are clever," he says, "and always alert. If a rabbit doesn't want you to catch him, then he'll disappear right before your very eyes."

"Your grandmother will never allow a rabbit in the house," my mother says.

"But couldn't we build a little home for him in the backyard? I'd feed it and keep it clean and teach it to do tricks," I say. "Pretty soon, everyone would love it and make it part of the family."

My father looks through the rearview mirror at me sitting behind him. "What if that rabbit didn't want to leave its own family in the woods? Don't you think its family might miss their brother or sister?" my father says, "Or what if that rabbit was some baby bunny's mother?"

For a few blocks I sit quiet and still, thinking about that rabbit and its family. I swallow, hard and gulp-y, like I might cry. "What about when you go hunting and kill a rabbit?" I say. "Did that rabbit let you catch it? Did its family stay up all night worrying when it didn't come home?"

Now my father doesn't say anything. He turns the last corner, steers the car into the church parking lot, pulls into an empty space, and turns off the engine. My mother looks at herself one more time. Then the three of us get out of the car and walk together into the sanctuary.

Everyone Lies about the Truth and Other Things My Father Said

- If you fix something yourself, you'll feel better than if someone fixes it for you.
- Tell the truth. For as long as you can.
- Sometimes you have to bluff.
- If you catch a fish, either let it go or eat it, no matter how bad it might taste.
- Sometimes there's no danger to watch out for.
- You don't have to fry your bologna to make a good sandwich.
- It's okay to swim in the rain. You're already wet.
- You are part Cherokee, maybe the best part.
- In the war I spent Christmas on Easter Island.
- My dream was to own a diner.
- Sometimes you have no choice but to tell a lie, but at least be sorry about it.
- You can be happy inside without laughing out loud.
- The fish are there even if you never catch one.

- Even the smartest person can get lost. Smart people don't stay lost.
- Find the best in someone, especially in yourself.
- When I was a boy, I got lost in the woods eight times. Every time, I found myself.
- My mother could barely read, but she still told us stories.
- A good hunter learns to be quiet inside himself.
- Always look behind you before you cast your line.
- The truth won't always set you free. Sometimes it gets you in trouble.
- When I was a boy, I told my mother I wanted to run away. She said I could, but I'd have to take my little sister with me.
- Cowboys and soldiers in movies look too clean to be real.
- Sometimes you have to take a chance.
- A good hunter knows when not to take the shot.
- If you know someone lied to you, try to understand why.

The Digging of Small Holes

My grandmother and I are making another one in the earth. It won't take long with both of us moving the easy dirt.

My grandmother says, 'Someone should've stopped you.'

I don't say a word. My throat is full of sorry

She clucks her tongue, shakes her head, sighs heavy. I hear her judgment staring into me. 'Should've stopped yourself,' she says.

But I didn't. I'd saved my birthday money, waiting for the perfect purchase.

And then in the pet store I'd seen the chicks. I'd heard their happy cheeping sounds, had wanted to sing along with them. They were dyed bright colors like Easter eggs. Sunny orange. Springtime green. Pink as bubblegum. Soft. Feathery.

A crowd of kids, even parents, scooped the tiny fluffy bodies up into their hands and petted them. Other parents dragged their grumbling kids away, leaving chick-less. I elbowed my way in. No parents nearby to stop me, and my grandmother next door at the beauty parlor having her hair curled for what our church called, Resurrection Sunday, the only day besides Christmas when she goes to church.

The sign said, *$1 each. 3 for $2.50*. I had more than enough. The helper, a teenager I recognized from church, handed me a cardboard box. 'When you get home poke air holes in the top,' she said, 'for breathing,'

In the glass display case, dozens of biddies crammed together so catching them was quick. I captured three—pink, turquoise, purple—and settled them inside my box.

At home, I gave them water and food that the helper had said to buy. I cut small holes in the box lid. When I woke up the next morning the purple and the turquoise ones had poked their heads through the air holes, trapping and choking themselves. Their tiny necks twisted. Their tiny eyes dull with death. I held onto the living one, the pink curve of it warm in my hands. I cried for them and for myself.

My grandmother and I dug a hole in the ground, buried the two babies together. 'If you keep that other biddy in the box, it'll die, too,' she said.

She rummaged around, found an old crate, slats wide enough for breathing, small enough for holding in the chick. It still looked beautiful, pink as a ballerina.

But now it's dead, too. 'From the dye,' my grandmother said. She eyed me till I felt smothered.

Now my grandmother and I are on our knees, digging earth for my last baby chick. Dirt sifts through my fingers, soft as feathers.

Her View of Forever

My mother hands my father something wrapped up in a tissue. She tells him to go into the pawn shop and borrow money so she can rent a room for a week at Windy Hill Beach where he won't even be with us. She tells him to get enough for a place on the oceanfront with a view that goes on forever. What's the use of a room blocks away where you can't hear the sound of waves? What's the use of a room where you're not even close enough for the sea breeze to frizz your hair? What's the use of a room too far away for my grandmother to walk to the water? My mother says all of this while we're waiting in the car. We wait a long time.

"When's he coming back with the roll of dough?" I say.

"It's not ladylike to call it roll of dough," my mother says.

You're not a gangster," my grandmother says. She sits next to me in the sticky hot back seat, blotting her forehead with her handkerchief. "Rich society people would say, disposable cash."

"No, they wouldn't. That sounds trashy," my mother says. "At the bank we call it, available funds."

"Wouldn't it have been easier to get some available funds while you were at work?" I say.

My mother laughs her nothing-is-funny laugh, dry and scratchy like something is stuck in her throat. "Working in a bank doesn't mean you have money there," she says.

"How do you get money from a pawn shop?" I say.

"It's like a loan. You give them something you aren't afraid to lose in case you can't pay them back," my mother says. "Something that doesn't matter to you."

"It might matter more than you think," my grandmother says.

My mother doesn't say a word.

When my father finally comes back to the car, he hands her an envelope. My mother looks inside, counts the bills, makes a little lumpy noise. No one says a word all the way to the Chevrolet dealership where my father works in the service department. He gets out. My grandmother moves to the front seat, and we drive away, leaving my father alone on the sidewalk. I stick both my arms out the window and wave, but he doesn't wave back. His hands are buried in his pockets.

"Keep your hands inside," my grandmother says. "I knew a girl whose arm was sliced off her body when a truck went speeding past her family's station wagon."

I pull all of myself into safety.

It takes hours to get to the beach. We ride along back roads, passing fields and shabby abandoned farmhouses almost swallowed by vines. Even with all the windows rolled down, my grandmother and I are red-faced and soggy with sweat, but not my mother. She's cheerful and crisp and looks brand new in her pink shorts and matching blouse with tiny buttons shaped like seahorses.

Finally, we see the ocean and smell salty air. I point to five different motels with vacancy signs, but my mother keeps driving until she sees one that suits her.

"Perfect," she says, pulling up to the Sand Castle Inn, whose sign says, *Grand Opening*. "We'll have a room with beds that nobody has ever slept in before," she says, "with pressed sheets and fresh towels whenever we want them."

My grandmother shakes her head and looks at me. "Even so," she says, "I'm checking for bedbugs, and I'm cleaning the toilet before anyone sits on it."

"You won't need to clean. I'm getting a brand new room," my mother says, "with a brand new toilet and bathtub. We deserve the best of the best."

"Germs live everywhere, even on brand new toilets," my grandmother says, flaring her nostrils. "You can die from anything, anywhere, anytime. Nobody is sitting on the toilet until I clean it."

"What if I have to pee really bad?" I say.

"Ladies can hold it forever," my mother says.

"But what if I can't? What if I have to pee so bad that I wet the brand new floor?" I say. "Can I squat over the toilet? I won't let my fanny touch the seat."

"Ladies never squat," my mother says.

My grandmother looks at me and shakes her head. "Even ladies have to squat sometimes," she says. "They may not want to. They may have thought they'd never in their life be in that awful position, but here they are, reduced to the lowest of the low, the humblest of the humble, the poorest of the poor."

"Well, today we are neither low nor humble nor poor. We have available funds," my mother says. She opens her purse, digs around for her lipstick. Then she tilts the rearview mirror so she can see her face. She pinks her lips, smiles at herself, drops the lipstick back into its rightful place, and gets out of the car.

I scramble out of the back seat, but she stops me, jutting out her hand like a traffic cop. "Wait here, Retta," she says. "You're too crumpled and damp to make the proper impression. We wouldn't want the management to think we're riffraff."

She fluffs her hair. That's when I notice that her marriage bands are missing.

"Where are your rings?" I say. My grandmother huffs.

"It doesn't matter," she says. She shoos me back into the car. I climb into the front seat behind the steering wheel. My mother takes the envelope stuffed with the roll of dough and disappears into the Sand Castle office.

I look at my grandmother, slumped and worn from the heat. "If I could drive," I say to her, "I'd take us over the dunes and down to the water where the breeze would cool our skin and the sand feels soft and we can see the endless ocean."

"Nothing is endless," she says. "Not even forever."

And there we sit, stalled and sweaty, until my mother returns holding the key to everything in her hand.

My Grandmother Steals Oleanders at Windy Hill Beach

My grandmother can't abide the August scorch, the gritty itch of sand, the buzz of mosquitoes and green flies. She won't even snooze under the beach umbrella my mother bought on sale at the souvenir shop. Most likely, it's the worst week of the summer for her, maybe even the year. She wrings her hands at the very thought of my building a sandcastle or playing in the waves.

"A minefield for bare feet, that's what this beach is. Broken glass. Barbed fishhooks. Stranded jellyfish that will sting you into the emergency room," she says. "And don't even get me started on that ocean, how it waits for you to step into its dangers. Riptide. Shark attack. Drowning." She scowls and shakes her finger in my face. "All that's left for me to do is worry-watch for the certain death of my only grandchild."

"I'll be fine," I tell her. "I don't even go out past my waist, and I'm not very tall so that's hardly deep at all.

If you'd come down to the water, you'd see how fine I am."

But she doesn't. Instead, she haunts our motel room, pacing back and forth and watching for waterspouts and tsunamis. The only pleasure she has are her flower jars which she brought from home and now has lined up on the tiny balcony. She frets and waits for my ocean time to end and afternoon heat to chase my mother and me off the beach and into the air-conditioned room.

While my mother paints her toenails or naps or reads fashion magazines, my grandmother arms herself with scissors and damp paper towels and wanders me out to steal oleanders. We stroll a few blocks inland into neighborhoods where people live all year, places that lowly renters who only borrow the beach usually don't see.

"Look like you belong," my grandmother says, so I whistle. "Proper people don't whistle," she says. "That's a dead giveaway that you aren't fancy enough to fit in here."

I stop and hum instead. Hymns. They are always ladylike, especially *Amazing Grace* or *America the Beautiful.* My grandmother hums along until she spies some unsuspecting oleander flowers.

"Over there, next to the porch. Off you go. Sneak quiet. Side-scuttle like a crab," she says, scrunching herself down behind a hedgerow. "Mind you don't put them in your mouth. They're poisonous."

"I'm old enough and smart enough to know not to eat plants," I say.

"You're never too old to be polite, and you're never too smart to be reminded of danger," she says. "The smartest people stay wary, especially of beautiful things that can lure you into certain harm. Now, get on with you before someone shoos us away."

I take off silent as a shark while she keeps lookout. All the while I keep my eye on the door and windows, spying for quick movements inside the house, hoping nobody catches sight of me edging my way toward their bushes and shrubs. When I get to the oleanders, I make myself small, hunching down, imagining I'm invisible. Then I snip the stems, on a slant, near a node, exactly like my grandmother has taught me, picking ones with new leaves and delicate blooms.

I head back to her, my hands full of oleander cuttings. Then in the damp towels she brought, she wraps them tender, like she's diapering a baby, cooing like she's hushing them to be calm.

Back at the motel, she freshens the water in her rooting jars. "Imagine the whisker sprouts we'll have in a few weeks," she says. "I'll green-thumb these shoots until they're tall and happy in my own backyard. They'll grow up fine and never miss the life they would've had here."

I look at my mother propped up on fluffy bed pillows working her crossword puzzle, and I know she'll miss every single second of this life that she's imagined for herself.

The Teeth of Sharks

Once, my father went to the beach with us. We stayed at an old house that had survived two hurricanes though it looked like it hadn't. My father got the house for free because his friend, Red Eye, was half owner, sharing it with his brother.

My father had said it was nice, oceanfront, and we should be grateful. My mother had said she'd make her decision on that when she saw it with her own eyes.

All the way to the beach she complained about my father's driving. He did drive fast around corners and when he stopped, it was like he was making an exclamation point. And we stopped four times on the way. Once for gas. Once for my grandmother to make sure she'd packed her medicines and hadn't forgotten her coin purse. Twice for me to go to the bathroom because the first place was too dirty for a lady.

We finally pulled into the driveway of a weathered old house. It wasn't painted a pastel color like other cottages we'd passed. It didn't have a sign with a funny name like *Good Tidings* or *Fishy Business* or *Shore Do*. Instead it looked haunted, like it should've been named *Yikes* or *Run Away*. My mother gasped.

Red Eye's brother was there to give us the key. He and my father shook hands. They chatted until my mother and grandmother and I got out of the car. My grandmother told Red Eye's brother that the house looked dangerous.

"It's sturdy as Noah's ark," he said.

"It's leaning like it's about to sink," she said. "We could wake up tomorrow and be dead. I knew a family who died on this very beach when their house collapsed in a tidal wave."

"That's an old wives' tale," he said. "This house is fine. Roof's built on a slant. On purpose. Like a race car. Wind sweeps right over it. Whoosh."

My grandmother huffed at him, but he just smiled and told us to enjoy ourselves.

The inside of the house wasn't as shabby as the outside. The kitchen was painted sunny yellow, the other rooms, turquoise. Hanging everywhere were pictures of seahorses and lighthouses, dolphins and sandcastles. Tables were covered with conch shells, driftwood, and black, shiny sharks' teeth. Dozens of fishing poles, bait buckets, and nets filled the corners. The furniture sat cozy and soft. Stacked on shelves were books, games, baskets holding balls of yarn with knitting needles stuck in them like they were waiting for someone to make a sweater.

"This is the prettiest place I've ever seen," I said.

"My eyes can't take this much tacky confusion. I'm going to the beach where I can't see what you've brought us to," my mother said. When she talked, her teeth clicked like they were biting every word. She put her purse down, took off her shoes, and headed out the door.

"We need to clean the bathrooms and kitchen immediately," my grandmother said. "I can feel the germs crawling into my skin. We could all get scabies or worse."

My father brought in the suitcases. Then he grabbed some fishing gear and disappeared. My grandmother and I disinfected every inch of the house that we could reach.

Finally, I was allowed to go outside, though my grandmother said I shouldn't be in the ocean past my knees until my mother was there to save me in case a riptide washed me away or a school of sharks appeared to devour me whole. I wanted to say there was no way my mother could save me since she could barely swim, and even if she could, she wouldn't want to get her hair wet, but I knew better than to backtalk.

I changed into my bathing suit and walked outside. The tide was low so the strand was long and damp-packed. It was late in the afternoon. Almost no one was left on the beach. I scanned the water for the fins of man-eating sharks but no danger appeared.

I found my father shore fishing, standing with his feet in the foam of waves that had come and gone. He was facing the horizon, casting into the wide blue of the ocean.

"Where did you get these?" I said, bending down to dip my finger into a bucket where his bait minnows swam. I felt the tiny fish nudging me.

"I found them in that tidal pool," he said, pointing to where the water had collected. "Look for yourself. You might be surprised at what you can find even in the lowest of places."

I walked over. The water had almost all disappeared, either eased itself back into the ground or evaporated into the sky. A few unhappy stranded minnows flopped on the sand. I scooped them up, carried them back to the ocean where they could be alive.

Far, far down the beach, I recognized the shape of my mother walking back toward our shabby place. I waved my arms, hoping she'd wave back, but knowing she probably wasn't intent on the small speck of me. I went to meet her anyway. With every step I kept my eyes alert for the lost teeth of ancient sharks, searching for a perfect one—shiny, black, and sharp.

The Sweetest Taste

My grandmother and I go to the counter in the department store where they sell fruit-shaped marzipan, special chocolates from Switzerland, and hard candies like jewels: emeralds, rubies, sapphires. My eyes are overcome and I'm smelling so deep that my nose could burst from delicious pleasure. My happy breath fogs up the glass on the display case so my grandmother nudges me to step back.

She opens her velvet coin purse, counts out her saved money, and buys chocolate-covered cherries for me and, for herself, her favorite coffee candy wrapped in shimmery gold foil. She pops one into her mouth.

"Can I have one?" My voice is already oozy and thick with the thought of chocolate.

"Coffee isn't for children," she says.

"I'm almost a teenager now. Besides it's probably not made with real coffee."

"It most certainly is real coffee from a faraway country," she says. Her lips smack. "Coffee is not for young ladies. It will stain your teeth, make your fingers fidget, and your heart beat too fast," she says. I hear the candy clicking against her teeth. "Too much can kill you."

"Won't it stain your teeth and fidget your heart until it kills you?"

"I'm old so it doesn't matter," she says.

"Can I have your coin purse when you die from coffee?".

"I'm not dying anytime soon," she says.

"Everyone dies," I say.

""If you don't smoke or drink strong liquor or keep company with rough boys, then you won't die anytime soon either."

I don't tell her it's too late. I'm already hypnotized by the rough boy who lives next door. His eyes and hair are deepest dark like candied coffee.

When we get home I see that boy pushing the lawn mower into their backyard so I take my chocolate cherries and climb faraway into the tree nearest the fence where I watch him while he cuts the grass. Faded jeans. Sweaty t-shirt. Barefoot. My grandmother always worries that he'll back up the mower and chop off his toes. Even footless, I'd still adore him.

I'll never tell her that my fingers fidget and my heart beats too fast whenever I watch that boy, but that I could die happy if he noticed me high in that tree—fearless and waiting.

I watch him moving across the velvet grass, and I bite into the deepest dark, into the sweet, warm melt.

The Nest of the Rabbit

My grandmother and I set out to plant irises in our backyard beside the shed where the sun shines almost all day. We're on our knees, ready to turn over dirt and make a flowerbed, but her hand stops in midair. I look down and see an opening in the ground. A tiny tunnel. My grandmother digs enough to see that babies are nestled inside.

"What are they?" I say.

"Rats. Squirrels. Foxes," she says. "No matter what they are, don't touch them. I knew a girl who was bitten by a rabid raccoon," she says. "She had to get shots in her belly. She survived, but whenever she got excited, she foamed at the mouth."

We drop our gardening tools and head to the house.

"Call *That Father of Yours* at work and tell him to cancel his *important evening plans* and come straight home to deal with varmints." When she says this, she sneers a little because she knows he never comes straight home from anywhere.

Carolina, the lady who always answers the phone at the dealership, recognizes my voice. She asks me if I'm all right because I don't call unless there's trouble at home. I tell her we have varmints. Carolina says she'll page my father right away.

My grandmother plops into her rocking chair like she's set to have a fainting spell. "Oh, lord," she says. "We'll be shamed all over town."

"Why?"

"Nice people don't have varmints. Varmints in your house means you're the lowest of the low. You should've said we had unexpected company."

When my father comes to the phone, I tell him we have an unexpected company of varmints in the yard and that we're probably going to have to shoot ourselves in the belly with anti-rabies medicine so we won't over-foam from our mouths.

He tells me not to worry and that he'll take care of it when he gets home.

"It will be hard to see them after midnight in the darkest dark," I say. "Maybe you could come home sooner than usual."

My father says almost nothing in an almost invisible voice.

But before the sun goes down, he appears at home. I go with him into the yard to uncover the nest of badgers or ferrets or hedgehogs. We kneel down next to the little burrow. My father shines a flashlight onto a cuddle of babies. He smiles. "Not grizzly bears or lion cubs or even skunks," he says. "It's rabbits, barely born."

"I've always wanted a rabbit for my magic act. Can we keep them? Are they orphans?" I say, craning my neck to see into the nest. "They're naked."

"Rabbits are born without hair. They're probably not orphans. Usually the babies are left in their nests alone all day," he says. "The mothers only come home at dusk and at dawn so that they don't draw attention to the nest from predators. The babies are blind and helpless but these probably aren't abandoned."

My father and I sit on the ground together. "How do you know all this?" I say.

"Good hunters know the way of animals," he says. "It's important to keep a knowledge and a dignity if you're taking part in the cycle of their lives."

"Where's the mother now?" I say.

"Probably headed home for the night, but she won't come if we're here," he says.

"What are we going to do with them?" I say.

"We're going to leave them be," he says.

Back in the house, we watch from the back porch. Finally we see, from the far corner of the yard, the mother rabbit returning to the nest.

"The babies are okay. For tonight, everything's normal," I say. "What about the father? Will he be here soon?"

"The father of the rabbits doesn't come home at night," he says.

We walk toward the kitchen where my mother and grandmother stand shoulder to shoulder at the window, watching the day sliding down into dark.

My Mother in the Smoke

When she comes home from the fire that started in the break room at the bank, her hair, dress, even her shoes smell sooty. Her face is ashy gray.

"You could've burned to death," my grandmother says. "Thank goodness you were saved from a fiery death."

"The bank wasn't so lucky though. It's thick with fumes and drenched from the hoses," my mother says. Her voice comes out scratchy like it's been scraped. "So much is lost forever."

"Did all the money burn?" I say.

"Not all. The vault's fireproof," she says.

"Too bad the whole building wasn't fireproof," I say. "Is the bank forever doomed?"

She doesn't answer. My grandmother and I trail her to the back porch and watch while she slips out of her dress. She drops it into a stinky wad.

"That's your favorite," I say.

"Not anymore," she says. She stands there for a minute, her head bowed like she's saying it's funeral prayer.

The dress is my favorite, too. I love the color—darkest eggplant. Almost black but not a sad black because happy yellow and lavender pansy faces bloom on the sleeves and along the hemline, and the buttons are tiny flowers.

"Let's wash it," I say.

"It can't be saved. It'll hold the memory of tragedy."

"A tragedy for sure," my grandmother says. "If the bank closes, you'll lose your job." Her voice quivers. "Then whatever will we do?"

My mother passes us, again not answering. Even without her dress, her odor carries loud. I hold my breath until she disappears into the bathroom to wash away the fire. When she comes out, her hair is wet and her face is clean, but her voice still sounds husky and sore.

***

Every morning, my mother calls her supervisor hoping the bank is opening but, so far, only essential employees are allowed inside. My mother isn't essential.

She misses her regular customers, coffee breaks with her friends, wearing pretty dresses. She misses being out of our house. Here all she does is work crossword puzzles. She doesn't even curl her hair.

***

Finally the bank has its grand reopening. My mother wears her blue suit and pearl earrings that she saves for special occasions. She leaves the house extra early, which she never does. My grandmother and I watch her walk to the car. As she drives away, she waves like she's in a parade.

She's smiling when she comes home, her face shows no trace of ash, but when she walks by, she leaves behind the tiniest whiff of smoke.

That Day in November When No One Is Ready

I don't like for my mother to pick me up after school. She drives into the pick-up circle where all the seventh graders can see her old black Chevrolet. I know she hates that car, too, but not as much as I do. The other kids make fun of it, saying that it's so old it should be in a museum, that my father should've gotten a better car since he works at the dealership.

I've asked my mother to pick me up on the corner, but my grandmother told her it wasn't safe for me to leave the school grounds because escaped convicts could be hiding in the bushes, waiting to grab me and drag me away.

So after the last-period class, I usually hang around in the hallway, go to the restroom, rearrange books in my locker. Then I walk to the pick-up circle, hoping most kids have left.

Today was different. I went straight to meet my mother.

Today the President died. We found out during seventh period, Miss Whittier's class, while we were taking a test, filling out the names of African countries.

I hadn't studied or memorized anything. I only knew six, for sure. The rest I was guessing or making up: French Canelopia, Monolo Province, Niberia.

My mind hasn't been on schoolwork. I've been too busy thinking about the Thanksgiving holiday next week, and the fact that no one asked me to the dance the week after that. The popular girls in my homeroom whose families have shiny cars and big houses all sit together at lunch and whisper about boys they like.

They were doing that today before the President died. I could hear them talking about what dresses they'd wear and whose parents would drive them to the dance and which boy was the cutest. It was William, they all said. William, the seventh-grade president. William with blond hair and dreamy blue eyes and the dimple in his chin. William who likes Rebecca.

Both of them were in my class, Miss Whittier's Social Studies, when the loudspeaker came on. We heard the principal's voice crackle out. *Attention, students and teachers. We have important and tragic news. President Kennedy…*

He paused.

President Kennedy was assassinated today in Texas. All after school activities are canceled. Please go straight home after school. Let's take a moment of silence as we share our great loss.

Miss Whittier crumpled onto her desk, burying her face in her arms. I was close enough to see her shoulders trembling. The room was quiet.

Then William jumped up and hollered. *YES*. It was only one word, but it was a cheer. Like he was at a football game. Then, softer but like he was gritting his teeth, he said. *I'm glad he's dead.*

Miss Whittier lifted her head. She stood up. She turned her back on the class. Her shoulders slumped. Then straightened. I thought maybe she'd walk out and leave us alone, but she spun around, headed down the row to William.

Everyone was dead silent. No one moved. It was like we were afraid to breathe. Miss Whittier stormed forward until she towered over William like a storm. He lowered his face. His whole body collapsed into his chair.

Miss Whittier towered over him and her voice was a whispered thunder. "Do you know, William, what dead is, everlastingly dead?"

William mumbled that his grandfather died last year. His voice broke. He started to cry.

Rebecca leaned across the aisle. "It's okay, William," she said. "I'm not sorry President Kennedy died. My parents won't be either."

Miss Whittier looked at Rebecca. She shook her head. "Do you children understand what this means for our country?" she said. "What it means to have hope die?"

"I understand what it means," Rebecca said. "My parents say President Kennedy has the wrong ideas and that he's trying to ruin our lives, but now that he's gone, everything's okay."

Miss Whittier knelt down beside Rebecca's desk. She looked her right in the eye. "Nothing is okay," she said. "The President was assassinated. We're not okay."

Rebecca shrugged and turned her face away. Miss Whittier walked back to her desk and sat. Still. Silent. After a few minutes, she said, "Pass up your papers. The test is over."

I looked at my map, knowing I'd failed. Before I turned it in, I erased the wrong answers. Erased the guesses. Left only the ones I knew were correct. On the bottom of the page I wrote, *I am very sorry.*

When the bell rang, we left Miss Whittier, still sitting at her desk, crying. Kids were talking in the hallways, bunched together, until teachers hurried them along.

When I got to the circle, I saw William gesturing and talking loudly to a group of popular boys. He was telling the story of Miss Whittier falling apart. Telling how he and Rebecca made her cry. The boys laughed.

I walked by them and sat on the farthest bench to wait for my mother. I opened my book to the map of Africa, started memorizing the names of countries.

I sat for a long time until all the students were gone, until the teachers' parking lot was empty. The wind picked up. Dry leaves blew across the sidewalk. I thought maybe I should walk to the corner, where my mother might be waiting for me, but danger could be anywhere. So I waited. Finally, I saw her turn the corner into the circle. She drove slowly, the old car, black and sad as a funeral.

Bazooka Gum

In seventh grade it's important to have a boyfriend. All the popular girls have one, or they just finished with one and are on the lookout for the next. I tell that to my grandmother who is pressing shirts for my father. The steam from the iron wets her face so she keeps an electric fan on the table to blow on her.

"Don't stick your hand into the fan," she says. "I knew a girl who could've been a famous pianist, but she thought it would be funny to poke her hand in. All her fingers were instantly amputated."

"I don't play the piano," I say. "Everyone knows I'm a singer. I want to sing on big stages one day."

"Everyone knows that nobody will hire a singer who is a smart aleck," she says, "especially one who sasses her grandmother, and no boy wants a girlfriend who is snippy."

"Did you ever have a boyfriend?" I ask her.

"My father would not allow such foolishness," she says. "My sisters and I got a husband and that was it."

"Did you like your husband?" I say. I've never seen a photo of my grandfather. She doesn't talk about him at all. The only thing my mother says about him was that he was handsome, but I'm not even sure she remembers what he looked like.

"Yes, in a way. That didn't matter much back in those days," she says. She sprinkles the sleeves of a shirt, moves the iron back and forth, steam rising from the long arms.

"Why didn't it matter? People in movies and television shows act like that's all that matters."

"Because life was too hard to be all smoochy and lovey-dovey," she says. "We got married. The war came. The Depression came. He died. That was that."

"That's awful," I say. I want to tell her that's not going to be my life story. I want to tell her that I'm going to be a singer and marry a handsome man who doesn't die right off the bat, and that we'll have more than one baby who won't be allergic to me. I don't say any of that because I don't want to make her feel bad about her life. Also she'll tell my mother that I'm being sassy, and I'll be grounded.

"Well, if you never had a boyfriend, I guess you can't help me," I say.

***

I find my father in the driveway, under my mother's car. His tools are scattered around his feet and the radio is playing a football game. I scrunch down next to him.

"I need some advice," I say.

"Is it urgent?" he says.

"No, but it's important to my future," I say.

I hear him sigh, but he scooches out. His face and fingernails are splotched with oil.

"What kind of advice do you need?" he says.

"Romance," I say.

"Uh, oh. I knew this day would come." He shakes his head and says, "My advice is to elope. It will save us a lot of time and money. Who's the lucky boy?"

"I'd rather not say," I tell him. "Actually, I don't need romance help. I need to know how to tell if advice is good advice."

"Who gave you the advice?" my father says.

"A bubble gum wrapper," I say. "Bazooka."

"Well, a fortune cookie can get you into trouble. A Magic Eight Ball is nonsense" he says, "but I've never had a gum wrapper steer me wrong. What did yours say?"

I smile. I reach into my pocket and pull out the tiny folded paper. "It says, 'If you like someone, don't be afraid to say it or show it.' "

"Do you like someone?" he says.

"I do. He's funny and good at baseball, and I dance with him at Mrs. Bailey's Ballroom Lessons for Little Ladies and Young Gentlemen."

"Is he good marriage material? Would your mother approve?"

"I doubt it. He has a crewcut," I say. "I like him anyway."

"Then follow your wrapper," he says.

***

When my father finishes under the car, I ask him to take me to Woolworth's. At the jewelry counter, I use my birthday money to buy a bracelet and a heart-shaped charm like all the popular girls at school wear to lay claim to their boyfriends. I ask the clerk to engrave the name Bradley in curly letters.

***

On Monday I keep it tucked inside my sleeve, hidden all morning until lunch period. Then I let them see it, Lucy and Jeannie and the rest, and they race, prissy-running, to the boys' table to tell Bradley that his name is on my heart. I wait for the girls to run back, breathless and hot-cheeked.

"He likes you," Lucy says. "He sent you this." She hands me a rabbit's foot, fuzzy and soft and dyed bright green.

I hold the rabbit's foot, feel the luck gathered inside it, warm against my palm.

The Foot of the Rabbit

More than once, a rabbit has eaten my grandmother's violet leaves. She doesn't get mad. "Everything needs to eat," she says. "I plant a little extra. If the world was a perfect place, all creatures would have enough to eat, even if they have to eat each other. That's the way of it."

"Aren't you scared of being eaten by a tiger or gulped by a whale or attacked by a grizzly bear?" I say.

"In a thousand years I'm not going to be in any of the places where those animals might be feeling hungry," she says.

"But didn't you once know a girl that was eaten by some wild animal?"

"Don't be ridiculous," she says. "Things like that don't happen in real life. You watch too much television. I did once know a girl who watched so much television that she went blind and died when she stepped out in front of a bus."

***

"When your father cooks rabbit stew, I take a decent helping, but mostly I eat around the meat. Too gamy for my taste," my grandmother says. "I've nothing against the idea of eating what nature provides. It's not the preference of fine ladies, but life can turn on you. I've eaten all manner of wild food: dove, squirrel, deer. You never know what you might have to swallow when times are hard."

She tells me this while her hands are sifting through her fresh dirt and earthworms are wiggling through her fingers. I'm showing her my boyfriend's rabbit's foot and expecting her to be impressed at how lucky things have turned for me.

But it's not her reaction at all. "What a sad turn of luck for the rabbit," she says.

"Do you think someone ate the rabbit that owned this foot?" I say, feeling sorry now for the little animal.

"Let's hope so. Let's hope they were hungry and didn't eat around the meat," she says. "That at least it didn't die merely to end up as a trinket for silly children to claim as a prize."

***

When I examine my rabbit's foot to decide if it's real, I find the little claws. I push the fur away to see if I can pull them out, to see if they're plastic. I get out my grandmother's magnifying glass, take it into the bathroom where the light is brightest in the house, and look as deeply as I can. What I really hope to discover is that it's fake, that no breathing rabbit died and had its feet amputated so I could have good luck.

***

The next week at school, at the bike rack before first period, I see Bradley, standing with other boys from his baseball team. He doesn't notice when I walk by. I wave anyway and smile. Dangling from his belt loop I see a new rabbit's foot. This one is not dyed a bright color at all. It's tan and brown and looks like it came from a real, soft, life-breathing rabbit that maybe lived under someone's porch and ate from a garden of flowers and sweet green leaves shaped like hearts. And I wonder how many more rabbits' feet a boy like Bradley might have.

I Could Easily Ruin the Brand New Sofa

When my father's sister visits, I give her my bedroom. Then I have two choices. I either sleep with my grandmother in her too-small bed and scratch her back, or I sleep in the living room on the sofa that my mother just bought on credit at Davison's Furniture Store.

My grandmother likes for me to move in with her so she can watch to make sure I don't pass away in my sleep. "I knew a girl who died in the middle of the night from a nosebleed," she says. "It's dangerous to lie flat on your back."

I choose the sofa.

My father picks up Aunt Margie at the bus station and drives her home in a new demo car from the dealership. I run out to meet them. My father opens the door for her and helps with her big suitcase. She hugs me tight and long and giggly. I can smell her hair. Clean and spicy like cinnamon.

She hugs my grandmother and my mother, too, like it's the easiest thing in the world to do, and they hug back like it's perfectly normal, like we do it every day. Only we don't.

We eat dinner all together. Fried chicken, mashed potatoes, green beans, cornbread, and apple pie for dessert. Aunt Margie compliments every bite, gushing over how crispy the chicken is and how creamy the potatoes are. She tells my mother how much she likes her new lipstick and how pretty her bracelet is. She says that she'd like to take us all out for a fancy dinner tomorrow night or else cook her famous beef stroganoff. Whichever we'd like, she says.

Everything is as perfect as life can be, almost like a television show about a family who eats dinner together every night and whose mom wears lacy dresses when she dusts the piano and whose dad carries a briefcase and smokes a pipe and whose granny knits matching homemade sweaters and whose daughter makes straight As and sings solos in the school play.

After dinner we go into the living room. Aunt Margie fills us in on family news. I sit on the floor listening to her stories, but I can't get comfortable so I move to the sofa, next to my father. My back hurts. It's a strange ache that I've never felt before. I fidget a little bit longer, then excuse myself to go to the bathroom.

And that's when it happens.

Bright red drops in the toilet and on the tissue. My period. I know all about it.

My mother makes no secret of hers. She keeps her supplies in the bathroom closet. I've seen her attach the lumpy pads to her sanitary belt and position it between her legs a thousand times. I've seen her sit with the hot water bottle against her stomach or back. I've known her to call the bar to tell my father to stop at the store and bring home some pads.

I've heard my grandmother tell her she shouldn't embarrass him, and my mother say that he's the one who should worry about embarrassing someone. I've seen the plumber at our house more than once because the toilet is clogged with period pads that my father has begged her not to flush.

My grandmother doesn't have a period anymore. They stopped. "Good riddance," she said.

I stand in the bathroom with my pants off, wondering what to do next. I look in the closet, but the box of pads is empty. So I call out to my mother. "I need help," I say.

Without even a knock on the door, they enter. All three of them. My mother. My grandmother. Aunt Margie.

My mother stares into the toilet. "Seems like you're about to start your period," she says.

"Too bad," my grandmother says. "I was hoping it wouldn't be so soon."

"What a lovely surprise," Aunt Margie says. She looks down at my nakedness that I'm too stunned by their hovering presence to even try to cover up. "Yes, you're already well-feathered. So it's time."

"There are no pads," I say.

My mother rummages around in the back of the closet, but finds nothing. "I could send your father to the store," she says.

"Do you have any tampons?" Aunt Margie says.

"Of course not," my mother says. "Ladies don't use those, especially not children."

"What's a tampon?" I say.

"Nothing you need to worry about," my grandmother says. "I've heard terrible things about what happens with those. They're deadly."

"Let's just make do till the morning," Aunt Margie says. "Then we'll go out and buy some beginner pads. Until then, we'll use what we have, like the pioneers."

They find an old washcloth, fold it into a thick rectangle, and tell me to stuff it into my undies.

"What happens now?" I say.

"Not much," my mother says. "First periods are light."

"First periods are almost invisible," Aunt Margie says. "You won't even know it's there."

"I knew a girl whose first period turned into a hemorrhage, and she bled to death," my grandmother says.

I stuff the bulky cloth into my panties.

We go back into the living room where my father is sitting alone.

"Everything okay?" he says. His face has a strange smile that isn't really a smile at all, like the way he looks when my grandmother passes gas and no one is supposed to notice.

"Everything's fine," my mother says.

"Nothing will ever be fine again," my grandmother says. "It's the end of an era."

The rest of the night I'm very quiet. After everyone goes to bed, and I'm left in the living room all alone, I spread five bathroom towels on top of my mother's brand new sofa that isn't even paid for yet, hoping that I don't ruin it. I feel an oozing from inside myself. Then I lie awake, my stomach cramping in a new way that I'm not sure I'll ever understand.

What I Find Out about My Father

"Is beef stroganoff still your father's favorite dinner?" Aunt Margie says. We're walking to the store, just us two. I try to match my steps to hers, but I can't. She's tall like my father. Long-legged and lanky.

"I think so," I say. I don't want to tell her that I don't know what his favorites are, that he's not home much at night, that I don't see him very much except on the weekends when we go to church.

"I gave your mother my recipe," she says. "I bet she makes it all the time."

I smile. I don't tell her that my mother doesn't really cook at all, that my grandmother does the cooking and cleaning and laundry and the watching after me. I'm not sure why I don't tell the truth. My tongue seems stuck to the roof of my mouth.

"Maybe you can help me make it," she says. "I bet your father would love to know that you can rustle up his favorite dinner."

"That would be perfect," I say. "I'd love to make him happy."

Aunt Margie stops dead still on the sidewalk. She looks me straight in the face and laughs. "Oh, honey, you do that every minute of every single day," she says. "You know, when your father was married the first time, they were never able to have any babies. So when he married your mother, that was his dream."

I nod. I open my mouth to say something. My words stick. I nod again. I didn't know my father was ever married before. I don't know anyone whose parents were ever married before. I only know one girl whose mother is divorced, and my mother says she feels sorry for the poor, unfortunate, tainted woman, but Aunt Margie keeps talking like she doesn't think anything of it. She keeps talking as if she hasn't told a dark secret at all.

"Imagine how happy he was when he found out your mother was expecting a baby. And then imagine how happy he was when you were born, a sweet little girl with big green eyes and dark hair and the funniest little giggle." She takes my hand. "You've made him the happiest daddy in the world. That's what he always tells me."

My throat feels thick and full. I'm not sure I can speak without crying, but I try to act normal. "I know he loves me, that he loves all of us, and that we're a lucky family," I say, though sometimes I'm not sure of that at all.

Aunt Margie puts her arm around my shoulder. "Yes, you are," she says. "Sometimes out of an ending, a new beginning comes. Your daddy was low-down sad when he lost his first love."

She sighs deep and long. "Her death was tragic," Aunt Margie says. "It was before he went off to war. She died in a car wreck. Driving all by herself, early one morning on her way to work at the very diner he was hoping to manage and, maybe, buy one day. She died and his heart was broken."

My breath catches. I hate thinking of my father being sad and alone in the dark of dark.

Aunt Margie squeezes me close to her. "But he enlisted in the army and went for training and met your mother and that was that. Now just look how happy you all are."

I nod like I agree, but inside I'm lost to the wonderment of life and love and dying and lying and secrets and truth and how people sink and how they float, how there are people who smell like cinnamon and smile with their whole bodies and how others hold their breath and wait for the worst.

Aunt Margie takes my hand and off we go. She slows down, matching her long steps to mine. Deep inside myself I hide the talk between us, marking it as mine to keep.

If My Mother Really Loved Me, She Would've Had Sex with Gene Kelly

I could've been his love child with graceful feet that move like silvery raindrops. But my mother only danced with him once when he visited our town. She didn't offer him an evening of hospitality, winking so he'd understand what that really meant. I've spent a lot of time not getting over that.

My mother knows I'll never dance my way into people's hearts since she forbids tap lessons. "Ladies do not clickety-clack," she says.

"You can only take voice lessons. Besides, dancing leads to sex," she says, "and sex leads to getting pregnant and getting pregnant leads to being forced to marry a man who'll never be spectacular."

"But you let me go to Mrs. Bailey's ballroom lessons," I say.

"That's different. The boys there are from the best families and will grow up to be somebody."

"But you danced with Gene Kelly," I say, "and that didn't lead to sex or else I'd be singing in the rain.

My mother says if I use my singing talent, then someday I'll be a famous soloist for a television preacher. I don't want to warble like an old lady church singer. I'd rather sing with personality like Annette Funicello.

When my relatives visit, my mother wants me to sing "The Lord's Prayer," which I make into a medley with "Lipstick on Your Collar" in the style of Connie Francis. Someday when I compete for Miss America, that will be my talent.

My mother hasn't told me anything about sex. She just said it was bad and only the worst girls succumb, but my cousin told me the truth about sex. The good parts.

"Sex can feel nice and it's not gross. Well, it's sort of gross, but you get over that," my cousin says, "if the boy is dreamy.

"I'd rather not have gross sex, but if I have to in order to dance, then I'll sacrifice myself."

"Dancing doesn't make you have sex," my cousin says. "Dancing's just fun."

I beg my mother to take me to the movie theater where they're showing old musicals, but she said no. So imagine my face when, on Sunday afternoon, my father said he'd take me.

I never thought my father would go to see a musical. He's a mechanic, which my mother hates.

She hates his greasy fingernails. She especially hates his unspectacular crewcut.

The movie playing was *Singing in the Rain* with Gene Kelly. Afterwards when we were walking to the car, my father said his favorite part was when soaking wet Gene Kelly gave his umbrella away and danced in the rain. Then my father twirled himself around on the nearest streetlamp pole trying to dance like Gene Kelly, which was terrible. And wonderful. So I started spinning, too. We both laughed so hard and I realized, I was glad my mother didn't have sex with Gene Kelly.

My Grandmother Feeds Birds

Every day my grandmother makes cornbread like she thinks she'll get fired from her job if she doesn't. Every day she cuts off a chunk, slathers it with butter, wraps it up for my father to take to work for his snack. We always have leftovers that my grandmother feeds to the birds. My father says our yardbirds are so chubby that they can hardly fly. He says my grandmother makes them easy prey for neighborhood cats.

She says my father shouldn't insult the birds. It hurts their feelings. She says she knows a thing or two about hurt feelings.

When I help her cook, she rambles on about my father, clucking her tongue, calling him, *That Father of Yours.*

"*That Father of Yours* has no bird-sense. No woman-sense either," she says.

We mix cornbread batter and pour it into a sizzling cast-iron skillet. "*That Father of Yours* couldn't tame a bird if his life depended on it," she says while the cornbread bakes. "*That Father of Yours* is one mess of a man," she says while she's taste-testing a slice, hot from the oven, to make sure it's not life-threatening.

"I once knew a girl who served cornbread to her family without tasting it," she says. "The eggs were rotten. They all got food poisoning and died of unstoppable vomit."

"I almost die of unstoppable disgust when I see you ruin your slab of cornbread," I say, watching her crumble it into a glass of buttermilk. I squinch my face when she slurps and swallows. "Buttermilk smells rotten like it could kill you," I say. My grandmother slurps louder.

Every day we take the day-old cornbread outside. Right away, birds appear: finches, cardinals, phoebes, and her favorite, Girly, a female towhee that actually knocks on the window.

Smart birds don't get close to humans, my father says, but I think Girly is smartest of all, knowing where to get the best and biggest portions, free of dirt and bugs.

My father says birds actually prefer eating bugs, and, he says, no respectable bird would eat out of a person's hand.

When I tell my grandmother that, she harrumphs. "Girly and I respect each other," she says. "*That Father of Yours* should be so lucky."

Girly is best-loved because she has only one eye. My grandmother understands and worries over her blindness. She respects that Girly carries on in spite of it, landing on the kitchen windowsill, cocking her head, and pecking on the glass until my grandmother comes out with bread. In brood season, Girly brings her babies onto the porch and lines them up. Then she eats the bread and feeds her children by throwing up. Gross but amazing.

My grandmother feeds all strays, animals and people, because she learned a sad understanding of an empty stomach. Once there was an old yellow cat that showed up on our back porch. Skinny. Raggedy. A torn ear. Misery in its eyes. My mother said the cat probably belonged to somebody, but my grandmother said that cat belonged to nobody who cared.

She started feeding the orphan cat. She named it Chance because it needed a second chance or even a third one. Pretty soon Chance had a bed in the greenhouse that my father built for it and a little door so it could go in and out whenever it came home in the middle of the night. My grandmother said that was appropriate.

Sometimes my grandmother feeds Uncle Freeman, who is nobody's uncle. He has a bushy beard, a deep-chesty laugh, and tells jokes. He plays the spoons because he likes always having music in his pocket.

My grandmother makes me sing along with his tunes though harmonizing with spoons isn't easy. I think he's her best friend, but my mother says that wouldn't be ladylike.

Uncle Freeman rides the bus and gets the driver to stop right in front of our house. Then he shuffles across the street and taps on the windowsill a lot like Girly. Right away my grandmother goes to cooking. She bustles around the kitchen, starting a new batch of cornbread, pulling out leftover chicken or roast beef and cold buttermilk, and trying not to laugh at Uncle Freeman. The harder she tries, the more jokes he makes. Uncle Freeman told me it's a battle of wits. Then he said that was a pun, laughed, slapped his knee, and told himself that was a good one.

They sit for hours, remembering old times, complaining about old times, missing old times until my mother comes home from work, or I get back from school. Then Uncle Freeman tumbles himself out the back door and disappears for a while.

Sometimes when Uncle Freeman has been gone too long, I hear my grandmother whispering to my mother about him. What if he doesn't have a place to stay or he's back in the hospital? What if he's cold or hungry or alone on the streets like a scraggly old cat with no one to care? Then we pile into the car and drive around searching. We've never found him, and pretty soon, he shows up again, relieving my grandmother's worry.

I've asked my mother if Uncle Freeman is my grandmother's boyfriend. I asked if maybe one day they might get married and go on a honeymoon and live on a farm where they would grow their own flowers and take care of strays. I asked her if she thinks that, instead of living with us, my grandmother would be happier and not so scared with a nice husband who likes cornbread and buttermilk and feeding birds.

And my mother looked at me hard in the eye. "And what do you expect poor little Girly would do if your grandmother left?" she said. "That poor bird would have no one to feed her or her babies."

I knew then that my grandmother could never leave us, not even to be happy.

When Everything Starts to Tumble

Sometimes when my mother works later in the afternoon, I walk home from school. It's not that far, but the route my grandmother mapped out zigzags me through quiet neighborhoods so that I cross only one main road, and it has a traffic light to prevent me from being pulverized by a garbage truck. She knows how many minutes it should take me so she'll know exactly when to start being afraid I've been kikdnapped.

She'll be fine today because I walk faster in the cold January gray. It's almost drizzly. There's wet in the air. I hurry with quick, no-nonsense steps. Finally, I'm across the street from our house. That's when I see my grandmother sitting on the front steps. Stooped and without a jacket.

Usually, she'd want me to wait until she walks to the edge of the yard so she can make sure the bus isn't headed around the corner, but I don't stop. In fact, I run toward her. There are breadcrumbs scattered around her feet, but the birds have skittered away.

She lifts her head and looks at me with faraway eyes. Her words sound mushy. I drop my books and reach to take her arm. I get her inside the house and to her chair.

I take her face in my hands and look close into her. "Now, you stay right here. I'm going to call Mother," I say. "Don't you dare die in this chair where you rocked me when I was a baby. Don't you even think of doing that."

My mother answers her extension. "What's wrong?" she says, knowing I wouldn't call her at work unless it is urgent.

"You need to come home right away," I say. "Mama is sick." I hear my voice catch. I haven't called my grandmother Mama since I was little. The sound of it makes my knees bend, and I almost fall.

"Is she awake? Is she talking?"

"Yes," I say. "But she's making no sense."

My mother tells me she's on the way but that I'm on my own for now. I take off my coat and put it around my grandmother's cold shoulders. She looks at me and smiles, but only on one side of her face. I know something is very wrong because my grandmother never smiles on purpose. But her eyes are not as distant now as they were, and she's found a few real words like bird and hand.

In a few minutes, I hear someone coming in the door. It's Dr. Jamison, my grandmother's favorite doctor, the one she bakes a cake for with four layers and icing made with fresh-grated coconut every Christmas. His office is in his house and his house is close to ours. My mother must've called him right away. And here he is with his big black bag and serious doctor face. He shoos me away and takes charge.

He checks her over and says, "I'm taking her to the hospital. I can get her there faster than an ambulance."

We get my grandmother to his car. They're about to drive away, when my mother pulls up. "She's had a stroke," Dr. Jamison hollers.

"It's not ladylike to have a stroke," my mother says. "I'm sure it's just a nervous spell."

"It's a stroke," he hollers and orders her to follow him.

They all drive away and, for the first time in my life, I am alone, the only person in our house, the only person left to carry all the worry.

As If That Wasn't Bad Enough

We're lucky that my grandmother's stroke is mild, Dr. Jamison tells us. That she'll be mostly okay. No guarantees, of course, but she could be almost normal again.

I want to say that she's never been really normal, but I know better than to say anything close to that. My mother wants people to think we are the most normal family in the world.

So we get ready for my grandmother to come home from the hospital. We get a wheelchair, crutches, a bedpan, and a bell to put on her nightstand in case she needs us in the middle of the night.

In case there's a storm and the lights go out, I almost say out loud.

I want to pinch myself for being mean-hearted. I don't know why I'm so itchy and fussy, like I want to bite someone. I hate my awful self.

I want to be more like Aunt Margie who offered to drop everything and come to take care of us while my grandmother recovers. But I'm prickly, my grandmother would say, and if I stay that way, no one will want to be around me. I don't even want to be around myself.

Sometimes I sit at the hospital after school and keep my grandmother company. Sometimes Uncle Freeman stops by, too. He pats her hand and says, there, there, everything will be fine.

He tells her a joke or two, filches a saucer of jello, and off he goes before my mother arrives. That's usually his plan. Except for the one day that he's still visiting when my mother comes in. That changes everything all over again.

They have a cheerful talk about how happy they are that my grandmother's doing so well and will be home before we know it, cooking the cornbread and feeding the birds.

Then my grandmother lifts her head up and motions for my mother to come close. "Freeman doesn't have any heat," she says. "It's freezing this week. I wouldn't leave a dog in a cold room, much less a person."

"Don't you worry about me. I'll get by," he says.

"Nonsense," my grandmother says. "You go home now and when they leave, they'll pick up a bag of coal for you to burn in your stove." She tries to point to my mother but her hand flops.

My mother sighs and nods. "No one should ever be cold."

Uncle Freeman's eyes well up with fat tears. "You're the finest ladies I've ever known," he says. He gets his coat and scarf and leaves us three alone.

When we leave the hospital, it's heading fast to winter dark. My mother knows where to buy coal, and a man helps her load the bag into the trunk. We drive to a big old house that looks drafty and shabby where Uncle Freeman rents his room. It looks like it might cave in if just one more leaf falls on the roof.

My mother gets out, opens the trunk, leans in, tries to lift the bag, but it's too heavy for her. When she loses her balance, slips, and falls in, I hear her gasp and then groan. And then cry out when she can't get herself out of the trunk.

Uncle Freeman comes running from inside the house. He sees my mother crumpled in the trunk of the car. "Get help," she says.

He yells for someone to call an ambulance. And just like that, my pretty pink mother is headed to the hospital. Uncle Freeman and I wait in the parlor of the chilly boarding house for my father to find me and tell me that my mother's back is snapped and broken. Like the bones of a bird. A tiny fragile bird.

All of Us in the Same Boat

It's a warm Sunday in February. Warm enough not to use up all your coal if you live in an unheated room in a boarding house. Warm enough to be comfortable outside in the afternoon while the buttery sun melts over the backyard. Warm enough that the first pale green sprouts of my grandmother's daffodils poke through the soil.

When I woke up, my father and grandmother were in the kitchen, cooking breakfast. Together. Already bacon sizzled in the skillet. I came in and leaned against the counter while my grandmother talked my father through her cornbread recipe.

"How would you like your eggs?" he said.

"Scrambled," I said.

"Adam and Eve, wreck 'em." he said, smiling at his diner talk.

My grandmother shook her head at my unbrushed hair and pajamas. "Go make yourself presentable," she said. "You're supposed to be clean and tidy around food. I knew a girl who didn't wash her hands before setting the table and her whole family got sick and died of flesh-eating bacteria."

I looked at my father, but he kept wrecking my eggs. "Hurry up," he said.

When I came back, my hair, teeth, face, and hands were washed clean of family-killing germs.

"Order up," he said and handed me my plate. "Don't dawdle. Eggs aren't good cold." He poured the cornbread batter into the pan that cooked the bacon so the drippings could add their salty flavor.

After we ate, he called my mother at the hospital where she's in traction for her back. His voice sounded soft like the fur of a rabbit. He told her that we'd be bringing her lotion, magazines, and crossword puzzles.

While he talked to her, I watched him. Every move. Every detail. One hand holding the telephone, the other pushed down into his pocket. I watched him leaning his shoulder against the doorframe, crossing his long legs at the ankle, standing relaxed like he was fine being at home, cooking with my grandmother, chatting with my mother like they were happy and normal. I wondered at all the nights when he hadn't come home until late, late, after I'd been asleep for hours, after the house was darker than dark. I didn't care what had changed. Whether it was stroke or broken back or a lucky rabbit's foot, I was easy breathing.

Before he hung up, he told my mother that Aunt Margie would be here tomorrow to help out until we're all back on our feet again.

***

After we got back from the hospital, my father and I found ourselves in the backyard, staring at his car hood boat, covered up tight for the winter. We removed the tarp, dusted off the seats, shooed away the spiders. There it sat—shiny, hopeful, and waiting for spring—balanced on sawhorses next to the greenhouse where my grandmother was puttering around. We pulled over a ladder, and my father helped me climb inside. It rocked a little as if it was really bobbing on the surface of our favorite pond. He waited for it to settle, then slowly, gently, he lifted himself inside the boat with me.

We land-floated there for a while before we found the need for words.

Finally he said, "I know it's hard giving up your room for Aunt Margie."

"I don't mind," I said. "Aunt Margie brings us some normal, even if it's not real normal like most families have."

"Most families aren't normal," he said.

"Families on television seem normal," I said, "and happy. I want to be like they are."

"You aren't happy?" he said, like he was surprised.

"There's a lot I worry about," I said. "Strokes. Broken bones. Who knows what's next? I knew a girl who got seriously sick, and then her parents got divorced."

"You sound like your grandmother," he said. "Did the girl die? Did the world end?"

"No, she's okay," I said. "The world is okay."

We sat for a while, quiet as the invisible fish swimming under the car hood boat. My father looked up into the sky, his eyes searching the faraway blue.

"Someday we'll catch fish from this very boat," my father said, "but for right now, at least, everyone is fine enough, and nobody's sinking."

I imagined our family floating along, planning where to cast a line, hoping for smooth summer water with silvery fish leaping into the air, light reflecting a sparkle onto their scales, the sun warm all the way down to the bottom of the lake, down even into the darkest dark.

Acknowledgements

No flashy words can ever express my gratitude to everyone involved with the Bath Novella-In-Flash Award. Over the last several years I've had the pleasure of knowing and working with Jude Higgins and John at Ad Hoc Fiction to bring my two previous novellas to life. They've proved to be delightful, thoughtful, and knowledgeable. When my novella won the award this year, my overwhelming joy was enhanced with the certainty that, once again, I'd be working with them. It's been so lovely to find such cheerful, helpful, easygoing, and competent people. In their hands, I knew my novella would find a solid framework, an artistic appearance, and be treated with professionalism. Thanks also to Jude for her kind judge's comments. It means so much to be recognized in this way. This experience has been dreamy, stress free, and without any darkness in anyone's eyes.

Thanks to Michael Loveday for his cover remarks. He continues to be my inspiration as he brings new ways to explore flash and connect writers who love the genre. His coaching and counsel have made me a better writer.

Thanks to Ann Hood, my first fiction teacher at the Wildacres Writers Workshop, for her cover notes and her ongoing support and encouragement. Mostly, I'm grateful for the decades of friendship we share. A more authentic person you could not find.

Thanks to Bill Spencer for proofreading my novella. I appreciate his careful and watchful eye for detail and his patience with the fact that I love commas and often throw them in just for fun. Thanks to Carolyn Elkins for sharing ideas for the cover. Bill and Carolyn bring great joy to my life.

Without Wildacres Writers Workshop, Amy Burle, and my tribe there, I wouldn't be the person or writer that I am. The late director, Judi Hill, always insisted we read for no more than four minutes during open mic. That limit, I am certain, made me a better writer of flash. I'm fortunate to be part of the magic that happens each summer on the mountaintop at Wildacres.

Thanks to my family for ongoing support, shared glee as I find acceptances, and shared disappointment when rejections come. Thanks for being happily dysfunctional and solidly supportive.

My biggest thanks and unending love always goes to Jack McGregor, my patient husband, who listens over and over to the same stories as I edit and revise and edit again. Thanks to him for understanding when I completely ignore him because the characters in my head are demanding my attention. I appreciate the fact that my real life is happier than any story I could imagine.

Previously Published

Many thanks to the following publications in which these stories or earlier versions of them first appeared in print and/or online:

"In the Dark Eyes of the Rabbit"—*Reflex Fiction*

"In the Boat with My Father"—*Fictive Dream*

"My Grandmother Brings Coca-Cola"—*The Weather Where You Are, Bath Flash Fiction, Volume Eight*

"Holding on for the Dearest Life"—*Bath Flash Fiction Anthology*

"In the Darkest Dark She Takes My Sleep"—*Dandelion Years, Bath Flash Fiction, Volume 7*

"For Their Own Good We Spy on Our Neighbors"—*Dandelion Years, Bath Flash Fiction, Volume 7*

"The Digging of Small Holes"—*Tiny Sparks Everywhere, NFFD Anthology 2024*

"My Grandmother Steals Oleanders at Windy Hill Beach"—*Poetry Society of South Carolina Yearbook 2006*

"If My Mother Really Loved Me, She Would've Had Sex with Gene Kelly"—*Root, Branch, Tree, NFFD Anthology 2020*

About the Author

Debra A. Daniel is the author of two novellas-in-flash, *A Family of Great Falls* and *The Roster*, (Ad Hoc Fiction), a novel, *Woman Commits Suicide in Dishwasher* (Muddy Ford Press) and poetry chapbooks, *The Downward Turn of August* (Finishing Line Press) and *As Is* (Main Street Rag). She is a Pushcart and Best Short Fictions nominee, has been long listed and shortlisted in many competitions, and has won *The Los Angeles Review* short fiction prize and Fractured Lit Work/Play Challenge. She was twice named SC Arts Commission Poetry Fellow, won the Guy Owen Poetry Prize, as well as numerous awards from the Poetry Society of SC. Work has appeared online and in print journals and anthologies including: *Fictive Dream, Reflex Fiction, Flashback Fiction, Fractured Lit, Tiny Sparks Everywhere, The Weather Where You Are, With One Eye on the Cows, Things Left and Found by the Side of the Road, Legerdemain, The Los Angeles Review, Fall Lines, Smokelong Quarterly, Kakalak, Emrys Journal, Pequin, Inkwell, Poetry Society of South Carolina Yearbook, Southern Poetry Review, Tar River,* and

Gargoyle. She is retired from a career in teaching and now sings in a band with her husband and was once on Who Wants to Be a Millionaire.

Printed in Dunstable, United Kingdom

67165412R00078